Night of the long knives

AND OTHER MISSIONARY ADVENTURE STORIES

by Hugh Steven

Wycliffe Bible Translators

P.O. Box 2727
Huntington Beach, CA 92647

Photos by Hugh Steven

Third Printing March 1984, WBT U.S. Div. Printshop
Huntington Beach, CA 92647

© Copyright 1971 by G/L Publications
Printed in U.S.A.

Published by
Regal Books Division, G/L Publications
Glendale, California 91209, U.S.A.

All rights assigned to Wycliffe Bible Translators

Library of Congress Catalog Card No. 72-161037
ISBN 0-8307-0107-9

For: Wendy
      David
      Lee
      Karen

My finest critics and four golden
gifts from God who
shine brighter every day.

Appreciation

Because this is a book about children and children of Wycliffe parents, let me express my profound thanks to God for each Wycliffe family. Especially their sons and daughters who must sometimes learn too soon the hard realities of life.

To each of my colleagues who provided anecdotal material for stories in countries I could not personally visit.

To my collaborator, editor and typist—my wife, Norma, for her constant love, encouragement and valuable criticism.

Contents

Before You Go Inside

With eyes shining, a fresh-faced teenager once asked me if it was fun to write. "No," I said, "writing isn't much fun."

"Then why do you do it?" she asked, with a puzzled look.

"Writing isn't much fun." I said again, "but having written is!"

And then after writing this book I discovered I had to eat my words. Because, while it was still hard work (try it if you don't believe me), writing this book was all fun. Fun because I caught a forgotten glimpse of my own boyhood in Chaddy Stendal—a fourteen-year-old tousle-haired character who goes barefoot and fishes for the rapacious and dangerous piranha in a central Colombian lake. Come to think of it, the only similarity between Chaddy and me is that we both used fishing poles. All I ever fished for was trout in an old mill stream in Canada. And I had to wear tennis shoes.

It was fun because through the book I have a chance to show you that young people all over the world think and feel very much like you. That no matter where they live, the color of their skin or the language they speak, young people everywhere play games, have fun and share similar dreams and hopes.

But more important it was fun to show an adult world they don't have all the answers on how to live a life of faith. We can learn from teens and subteens what it means to meet God in a fresh new way. Why don't you look inside and see if I'm not right.

HUGH STEVEN

Mexico

Night of the Long Knives

They walked in single file through a forest of tall Mexican pines. Each carried a long curved machete cradled in his arms. Some carried muzzle-loading shotguns in their arms. Others, cans of gasoline. The off-white wool ponchos and wide black wool belts marked them as Chamulas.

This tribe is notorious for hard drinking, accurate marksmanship and fanatic dedication to preservation of their animistic religion.

Chamulas have resisted fiercely attempts by outsiders to investigate their stills or interfere in tribal matters. Mexican officials in Las Casas remember with icy fear the time fifty Federal soldiers were dispatched to investigate a tribal feud.

Two came back.

1

Tribal members who by outside influence or personality quirk decide to construct a different style house, wear western clothes or change their thinking regarding traditional views of Chamula religion are not tolerated. Chamula tribal elders exterminate them like rodents. Bible translator Ken Jacobs knows this. So do a hundred or more Chamula believers.

The Chamula Christians, however, have chosen to obey the teaching of the "Book of God" Ken has translated for them.* Since they know the Son of God, they no longer want to live as animals. Through reading the Scriptures in their own language, Chamula believers discovered a dignity and freedom they never knew existed. Personal relationship with Christ released them from fear, the grip of drunkenness, vagrancy and witchcraft. They chose obedience to Christ even though they knew the unwritten tribal law—to deviate is to die.

The trail the Chamula men took this particular night led to a small stick house that sat cozily in the middle of a cornfield. There the men arranged themselves in a semicircle directly in front of the hand-hewn plank door. Without a word, they took a firm grip on their machetes and cocked their shotguns. Xalic (Chay-lick), leader of the group, (an old man by Chamula standards, perhaps aged 40), squirted gasoline on the thick thatched roof.

Inside, five people slept in the darkness. Five-

---

*For a comprehensive up-to-date account of the remarkable development of the Chamula Church, see Hugh Steven's revised 1983 edition of *They Dared to be Different*.

year-old Abelina with her three sisters and 18-year-old Paxcu, a "baby sitter,' all slept in Chamula fashion—nude—with their clothes used as blankets.

At first Paxcu coughed in her sleep. It wasn't long before the acrid fumes from the burning roof stung her into consciousness. Realizing the house was on fire she screamed frantically to the children

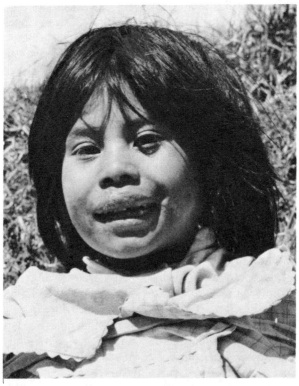

Abelina was only five years of age the night drunken men entered her hut and slashed her mouth with long knives.

to flee and she pushed aside the plank door.

The moment Paxcu's head appeared in the doorway, Xalic shot point-blank at her face. Twenty-one lead pellets tore into her face and neck and she slumped in the doorway. But just for a moment.

Through the horror her mind was still active. She knew she was alive and she knew she wouldn't be alive long if she stayed where she was. The long knives would be next. Paxcu gathered every ounce of strength and leaped into the bright moonlight night and headed for the cornfield. Xalic thrust out his hand to grab her. "It was because I was naked," she said later. "I just wiggled out of his grasp and flew into the cornfield." Miraculously Paxcu found the house of her uncle and survived.

Abelina and her three sisters were not so fortunate. Paralyzed by fear, they watched Xalic's ominous figure pass through the door. Then he paused to let his eyes become accustomed to the smoky darkness. The children saw the moonlight glint off his machete.

In the morning authorities, attracted by the fire, found the charred remains of one young girl in the smoldering ashes. As they poked around they suddenly heard weak moans coming from a coop-like structure nearby. Pulling open the door, they found three blood-plastered forms. Abelina, just barely alive, had a huge gash across her face and her left arm was hanging limp, almost severed. Only Abelina and her older sister made it to the hospital in Las Casas. Four-year-old Angelina died on the way.

Abelina carries a diagonal scar across her deli-

4

cate mouth, imprinted there for life by Xalic's machete. Paxcu's wounds have healed. She showed
only slight evidence of her ordeal as she and
Abelina disembarked at Chicago's O'Hare Interna-
tional Airport to take part in a Wycliffe Associate
banquet. They had made the trip unaccompanied.
Since the girls speak neither English nor Spanish,
the American Ambassador to Mexico sent an ex-
planatory letter to immigration officials in Chicago.

Little Abelina clutched a yellow stuffed dog and
gingerly allowed herself to be carried up the esca-
lator of the huge air terminal, into a world that had
not one shred of similarity with hers in southern
Mexico. It seemed hardly real that just a few
months before, in a police-type lineup, this little girl
had looked up into the hard face of Xalic and said
courageously, "You are the one who *killed* me when
I was standing in my little bed."

South America

I Don't Count Bubbles

Sharon Stendal brushed her long blond hair out of her eyes and draped it behind her left ear. Silently she watched a woman from the Kogi tribe of northern Colombia drop pebbles into a clay jug full of water. Four others sat around her in silence.

The stones were jagged and full of little holes. Each time the tangle-haired Kogi woman plunked in a stone, air bubbles rushed to the top of the jug. In a secret way, the woman counted the bubbles as they broke the surface. When the stones were gone and all the bubbles counted, she turned and spoke to Sharon.

"I have counted the bubbles," she said slowly, "and the gods have told me Ana will die."

Sharon's skin felt cold. A strange tingle of fear ran from the middle of her back right up to her thin neck. Moisture glistened in her eleven-year-old blue eyes but she held the tears. And instead of crying she yelled in fluent Kogi, "NO! Ana is NOT going to die!" She ran up the steep mountain trail to her own house. "I don't count bubbles. I prayed for little Ana and God is going to make her well," she reminded herself firmly.

The day before, no one dreamed three-year-old Ana would be almost dead. She had watched all day while Sharon helped her Bible translator parents pack and close up their small house. Sharon's mother and dad were leaving the Kogi tribe for a short rest and to take Sharon back to school.

Whenever Sharon's parents left the Kogi Mamarongo, dozens of long haired Kogis in their dull white tunics would walk several hours to see the big iron bird land and take the Stendals away. And like all the other times before, Ana and her friends were excited and kept asking Sharon when the big bird was coming, what was it like to fly in the air and wasn't she scared?

Sharon always answered their questions as if it was the first time they had asked. She explained the plane was supposed to come the next afternoon, but she didn't know for sure because the man who guided the bird thought the wind might be too strong to land on the airstrip. Sharon then told Ana and the others that she couldn't talk anymore because she had to check on her patients.

Sharon's mother had given her the responsibility of checking each day on people who were taking vitamin pills or other daily medication. It wasn't that Sharon's mother was lazy. It was just that the Kogi women would not take her seriously! For some unknown reason Sharon had the ability to make the Kogi mothers listen and obey her. Sometimes when Sharon saw a sick child playing in the rain, she would speak firmly but kindly to the Kogi mother and tell her that the child should be inside resting. And always the mother obeyed. But when Sharon's mother tried to explain the same thing, some Kogi mothers wouldn't even listen.

Then something happened that almost made the Kogis of Mamarongo *not* listen to Sharon. It was early on the morning Sharon and her parents were to leave. About 3:00 A.M. Ana's father banged on the Stendal's door and asked if they could come quickly and bring medicine for Ana. Mr. Stendal asked why. Ana's father explained with fear in his eyes that Ana had been stung by a scorpion!

In the morning, Mrs. Stendal told Sharon what happened during the night. She explained to Sharon that Ana began to rest comfortably after taking the medicine.

Without waiting for breakfast, Sharon rushed down to Ana's house. When she came back she reported that Ana was still sleeping and looked pale. "I told Ana's mother to keep her warm," said Sharon.

"We'll check on her a little later," said Mrs. Stendal. "In the meantime you can help me pack these last minute things. The plane should come by noon."

But by noon the wind was too strong for the

9

small JAARS plane to land and the flight was postponed until the next day.

"I don't know what we'll do," said Mrs. Stendal, disappointment showing in her voice. "We have given all our food away and everything is packed."

Then just when Sharon and her parents were feeling sorry for themselves because they couldn't fly out, they heard someone crying outside. It was Ana's sister.

Before the Stendals could ask what was wrong, she told them to come quickly because Ana was almost dead. When Sharon and her parents arrived at the small Indian house, they found Ana naked lying in a pool of cold water. Her once rich dark eyes were rolled back into her head and there was almost no warmth in her small body.

"What have you done?" shrieked Sharon.

"Ana had a fire demon that made her hot," said Ana's mother. "To get this demon out we covered Ana with cold water. It was because you told us to keep her warm that she got this demon."

"Ana must have started to run a fever," said Mrs. Stendal. "Sharon, run and bring a warm blanket and extra clothes."

While Sharon ran for the blanket and clothes, Mr. Stendal radioed the doctor. "The girl is dying from shock," said the doctor. "Keep her warm and give her a shot of cortisone."

"Where in the world will I ever get cortisone out here?" thought Mr. Stendal. Then he remembered a box of sample medicines that a doctor friend had given him. But then he thought, "What box is it

10

packed in? Where should I start to look? If I waste too much time, Ana might die before I find the right medicine."

"Lord," prayed Mr. Stendal, "I don't know if we have this medicine. And if we have it, I don't know where to look for it. But, heavenly Father, You do. Please help me find it."

Sharon Stendal knew the evil spirits could not make Ana ill—or well. But Sharon knew God could heal the child.

Mrs. Stendal looked up when Mr. Stendal entered the small room. "How did you get back so fast?" she asked.

"Well, honey," he said, "when you pray in faith the Lord really answers! I found the carton right on top of the first box of medicines I opened! And I put my hand right on the vial of cortisone! It was in that little box that you used to say was in the way all the time."

After Mrs. Stendal gave Ana the medicine and wrapped her in the clothes and blanket, the Stendal family gathered around and once again asked God to make Ana well. Mrs. Stendal stayed with Ana several hours and then left.

She came back to her own house and found Sharon boiling eggs on an open fire. "All I could find for supper," said Sharon with a twinkle in her eyes, "are a few eggs and some old soda crackers."

After supper Sharon walked back down the trail to check on Ana. When she went inside she opened her mouth to speak but couldn't get the words out. What she saw almost made her cry. Ana's mother was dropping stones into a clay jug.

Sharon ran home and told her mother what she had seen. "The only thing we can do," her mother said, "is pray and ask God to heal Ana. He is stronger than the evil spirits they worship."

Early the next morning Sharon and her mother walked down the trail toward Ana's house. With butterflies in her stomach, Sharon called out hesitantly in Kogi, "Are your eyes working yet?" Almost immediately the tiny plank door was pushed open and Ana stepped out smiling.

"Oh," cried Sharon, "you are better! You are better! God has made you better!"

The pilot taxied the blue and white single engine plane down the airstrip and stopped at one end to rev up the engines. The Stendals were ready to fly out.

"You know, Mom," said Sharon, "I was frightened yesterday when Ana's mother counted the bubbles and told me Ana was going to die."

"I was a little frightened, too," Mrs. Stendal admitted. "But isn't it great that we could show the Kogis the power of the true God!"

"I am so glad," said Sharon, "I don't have to count bubbles."

"Yes," her mother agreed, "and I think someone else is glad we don't count bubbles. Look out there. Isn't that little Ana waving good-bye?"

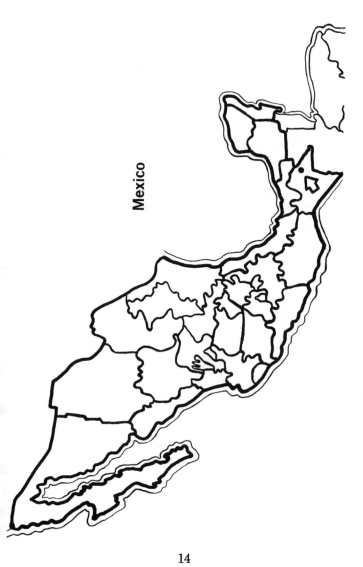

Mexico

14

The Forgotten Hoe

I am a Tzotzil Indian and I live near Las Casas City in southern Mexico. Most people think Mexico is hot. It is very warm in the lowlands. But in the highlands of the State of Chiapas where I live, the wind blows through the mountain pines and it is cold.

Tourists like to take pictures of me. They think it strange my people and I wear short pants and tie long ribbons to our hats.

Ah, but I did not come to talk about how I look or how cold my village is. I came to talk about my hoe.

"Antonio," said my wife one day, "where is your hoe? How can you weed the cornfield without your hoe?"

My hoe. Yes, yes. I remember now. I left it in the cornfield near Lencho's house. So I went to the house of Lencho and asked for my hoe.

"I am sorry," answered Lencho when I came to his door, "but your hoe is not here. Go ask at the house of my older brother."

So I went. When I asked about my hoe, the older brother said, "I don't have your hoe. My younger brother Lencho has it. I heard him say he would hide it if you came back for it."

So I went back and called to Lencho. "I hear you have hidden my hoe. Why would you do that? It is not a good thing that you have done. God's Word says that we should not steal."

"Oh, so you're an evangelical," said Lencho. "Just wait and I will show you what I am going to do to you!"

Lencho was angry and rushed into his house. In a moment he ran out with his gun and pointed it at me. "Our Municipal President has sent out an order that says whoever comes around and says he is an evangelical, we are to shoot him."

I did not like looking into Lencho's gun barrel but I said bravely, "It is true. I am a Christian evangelical. I have God's Word in my language. I found that God's Word is good and believing in Jesus makes me glad inside. Would you like to hear some of it?"

"I don't know," said Lencho. "I am not used to listening to such things. But I will listen if you tell it to me well."

"Listen then," I said to him.

"Go, woman," said Lencho to his wife. "Bring a

little stool for our visitor to sit on so he can tell us these words."

In a moment she brought me a stool and I sat down. "Now," said Lencho, "tell it well, the things you have to say to me."

"I will tell you what *God* has to say to you," I said. "It is God's Word. It is not my words."

"All right," said Lencho. "Say it then." When Lencho sat down to hear me speak, he kept fingering his gun but I was not afraid. "Just what is God's Word anyway?" he asked.

"God's Word," I said, "is the words that Jesus Christ Himself spoke. He said, 'If anyone believes in me he will not be destroyed even if he is dirty with sin.' For that reason it would be good if you would believe also. Because when we believe we

The Chenalho Tzotzil people in the state of Chiapas in southern Mexico, linger after a worship service to chat with Bible translator Ken Weathers.

leave off the things that are bad. We leave off stealing, lying and killing. We leave off arguing, fighting and evil desires, because God doesn't want those kinds of sin in our lives."

"Oh," said Lencho, "that is good." But all the time he kept fingering his gun, lowering it and raising it while I sat there. I wasn't afraid. I just said to myself, "God is in my heart. He will protect me."

Then I continued to talk. "Before there was a heaven or earth, God was there alone. He made everything there is. He made the light for the earth and sky. He made the sun, stars and moon. He made the rivers and all the water there is. Everything in nature is the work of His hand. When you and others don't know about God and His Son, Jesus Christ, you fight and become angry against the Word of God and God's people. It is natural for people to be thieves and say bad things when they don't know God's Word. It is sin that makes people believe doing bad is good."

"I used to think," said Lencho, "that evangelicals were bad. But I like what you say. I would like to hear more."

"Good, I will come and tell you again," I said. "In the meantime, think over what I said. If you believe you will find God's Word is good."

"Maybe it is so," he said. "I will think." So I told him good-bye.

When I returned to my house and told my wife, she asked, "But where is your hoe?"

My hoe? Why, I forgot about it. It stayed there!

South America

The Time Machine

When I returned from a trip to Colombia, in South America, I wanted to show my nine-year-old son, Lee, where we made a forced landing. But all I could find on the map was a thin, wiggly line that represented a river somewhere in the middle of Colombia's remote Vaupes jungle.

"Look, Lee," I said enthusiastically. "The heavy rain and wind forced us to land right—uh—about— here."

"Doesn't look like much of a place to me," he said with disinterest.

Lee reminded me that I had told the story several times before and wondered if he could go outside and throw some football passes to his older brother. "OK," I said, trying to sound hurt. But I knew Lee was right. I had told him the story of the time machine before. But I haven't told you and you might like to know how it goes.

It all began the morning I was scheduled to fly out of a remote village in eastern Colombia. The door on my side of the single engine, two-seater helio courier broke. But that didn't bother my trusty pilot, George DeVoucalla. With a nothing-ever-bothers-me kind of smile he expertly wired it shut. That was OK but it meant the only way I could get in or out was bending over, like I had been kicked in the stomach by a mule, and climbing in backwards from the rear seat entrance. All the weight had to be up front and at 210 pounds, George wasn't taking any chances with me. Besides, we had another passenger and gear in the back seat.

I practiced this strange contortion just to be sure I could do it. And I did it with a minor amount of difficulty. Of course if you ask the people who stood around to watch, they might tell you a different story. No doubt they are still laughing.

Just after George fixed the door and I did my acrobatic act, it started to rain. I went back to a little palm thatched hut, stood under the eaves, and watched the big drops of rain hit the river like thousands of steel marbles. A big green parrot squawked and flew out of the trees.

Almost as quickly as it started, the rain stopped. The rich blue Colombian-Brazilian sky was just waiting for us to come flying. And fly we did! Up over the jungle with two-hundred-foot trees that looked like clusters of broccoli tops.

At lunch time we landed in a small frontier town with the peaceful name of Flower Town. Everything looked normal until I noticed people in an eating place unbuckle their gun belts and hang them over a chair while they ate. I blinked my eyes and wondered if our airplane really was a time machine that had taken us back a hundred years to the old Wild West shoot-em-up days!

"It's getting late. We'd better get going," said George after we finished our meal of fried bananas, rice, yucca, green peas and piranha. "The sky looks a little strange. Hope we can make it back before a storm comes. I don't want to spend the night here."

But twenty minutes after we left Flower Town, we knew it would be impossible to get back to home base. Strong winds and pelting rain were pushing us around in opposite directions, like two boys blowing a ping pong ball around on a table top. At one point an up-draft shot us from 8,500 feet to a dizzying 11,000 feet. George, calm and full of confidence from years of jungle flying, brought the little plane under control. "I think we better turn back," he said. "I know a place where some settlers have an airstrip."

But when we reached the airstrip and descended for our landing approach, the crosswinds reached out like a giant's hand and held us back. Instinctively I braced myself for the worst. For a second it seemed as if we stood still. Then we started to fly sideways. Fortunately the helio is specially equipped to prevent stalling and can fly as slow as forty miles per hour. Just as I was wondering what would happen next, a strong gust of wind tilted the plane so that now I was looking almost straight down at the waving trees through the window in my wired-shut door! All I heard was strong wind and the roar of the engine as George opened the throttle and banked away from the approach.

For a long time no one spoke. Finally George said something about landing at a place called Two Rivers.

"What's at Two Rivers?" I asked.

"Oh, not much," said George. "It's a tiny rubber hunter's outpost near a spot where two rivers meet. It has about twenty-five or thirty men and their families who live in a big old jungle community house and hunt for natural rubber latex and resin for chewing gum."

"That's interesting," I said.

"What's really interesting," said George, "is that they have an airstrip so we can land! And there it is right down there."

Our landing at Two Rivers was normal and easy except for kicking up a strong spray of leftover rainwater on the wet strip. The plane skidded to a stop and I crawled up over my seat and through the back door. And then I felt it—the most glorious and wonderful of all feelings—solid ground!

"Thank you, Lord," I breathed, "for bringing us down safely." I wanted to shout and to skip up and down! Never did a wet, muddy airstrip look or feel as good!

When I looked around at the lonely outpost trading station I realized our time machine had brought us to an almost forgotten moment in history. The man in charge of the station, a small, barefoot, bushy-haired man in black, baggy pants, treated us like royal guests. He fed us a fine meal of yucca and piranha, with piping hot chocolate to wash it down. After supper he showed us where we would sleep. It was the finest room in the big community house—an old combination store and storeroom. Our beds were new rope hammocks that we tied to the pole rafters. I yawned, gave myself a push, swung back and forth and drifted off to sleep.

In the morning after breakfast of piranha and yucca, the same bushy-haired man asked us if we would like to take a short canoe trip.

"Might as well," said George. "The weather still is bad for flying. Probably won't clear 'til noon."

Smiling with happy excitement, the little man led us down a slippery riverbank to a long mahoga-

Our time machine had landed across the river from the school on stilts where the children were having recess.

ny dugout canoe. Then, from out of nowhere, a half dozen eleven and twelve year olds scrambled into the canoe beside us and sat silent except for an occasional giggle.

"Where are we going?" I asked.

Our friendly guide said something about a school but before I had a chance to ask any more questions, he guided the heavy canoe away from the bank and down the river. In a few minutes we docked on the opposite side and climbed up a high bank to a small clearing.

"Here is our school," said the little man proudly. It was a newer but smaller version of the community house where the rubber hunters lived—a big house set up on stilts with a palm thatched roof and bark walls. Inside a dozen children sat on crude handmade benches with tables as desks. The furniture, like everything else, was made from wood taken from the surrounding jungle.

Like the children in the canoe, these children were shy and at first a little frightened with so many outside visitors. But in a few moments, they dashed outside for a recess and promptly forgot all about us. They were more interested in looking after their pet monkeys and parrots and playing a riotous game that looked like a combination of soccer, basketball and American football.

The teacher, a young evangelical Christian Colombian woman from a city some distance away, showed us the courses she taught. The old-fashioned reading, writing and arithmetic books were wrapped in plastic to keep them dry and clean. In addition she taught two other important subjects—

Colombian history and personal hygiene.

"We have so many diseases here," she said, "and are so far from outside help that we must teach our children how important it is to clean their cuts and scratches. And also how they should boil the water they drink. We even have a raised firetable to show how to prepare food away from pigs and chickens. Many of the children who play so happily here today will die too soon because they will not practice the good health lessons they learn in school. Many, when they grow up, will die spiritually because out here in the jungle they have almost no chance to hear how much God loves them. How truly happy children in your country must be to have schools and churches close together to learn all the good things in life."

We said good-bye and left the school, with the children still playing their game. As we flew over the little schoolhouse in our 'time machine', I waved. They couldn't see me but they waved back at the high flying plane. And then we were out over the 'broccoli tops' on a two hour flight to home base.

"Our plane," I thought, "really is a time machine. It not only took me back to frontier towns, jungle outposts and Indian villages where people live and do things today just like they did hundreds of years ago, but it's taking me back to my own twentieth century world of moon rockets, TV, telephones, antibiotics—and back to children like Lee, whose world is sports, a brown and white beagle named Freckles and schools and churches close together."

Mexico

28

The Woollytown Five

Andy blew a long, loud, off-key blast on his trumpet and heaved a sigh of disgust. "Some audience," he said to nobody. "They didn't even turn around to see what happened."

The truth was they didn't care! The people just wanted noise. Loud noise and lots of it. This was Lalana at fiesta time and Andy and his five-man combo were the town heroes because they could give the people the noise they wanted.

Lalana, Mexico. The name means "Woollytown" but nobody seeing this scene would think of sheep. It was more like the "wild and woolly West" of the frontier days.

Three times a year—Christmas, Easter, and All Saints Day—the Chianantec Indians of southeastern Mexico gather for religious festivals. They take their images from dusty alcoves, decorate them with multicolored crepe paper and parade them around the village plaza. And that is when Andy and his Woollytown Five take to the streets.

But Andy's heart wasn't in the music this time. He smelled the odor of singed pig's hair, saw the copper pots of boiling meat, heard the women chattering as they patted out tortillas and heard the boisterous shouts of men who were already full of corn liquor.

"It will be just like all the rest of the fiestas," Andy thought as he watched the scene before him. "If the images are so powerful, why don't they move around by themselves? At least they should move their eyes or arms."

Disturbed by these questions, Andy left the fiesta to visit the Bible translator who had lived among the Chinantecs for the last three years.

"The only way to settle this once and for all," he told himself, "is to ask God Himself which of the two paths is the right one for me to follow."

And that is what Andy told Dr. Calvin Rensch he had to come to do. God's answer to Andy's question came through "The Paper," the Chinantec translation of the Bible that Rensch had been working on since his arrival.

Later, Andy said of this experience, "After listening to God's words, I believed His way was right. Now my heart is at peace." And Andy had played for his last fiesta.

The villagers did not like this and made threats; as time went on the warnings became encounters.

One day Andy found his path blocked by an angry village elder. "Since you have given up the images and will not play in the band or go to fiestas," the man shouted, "you and anyone who believes the foreigner's message must use the back mountain trails. If you return to the ways of our ancestors, you can use the main trails again. But we will lock you in jail if you stay on this trail now."

The conflict was now in the open. Probably it wouldn't have created such strife if only Andy had believed. But he had talked to the rest of his band and all four of them had come to faith in Christ. The villagers now had to find new musicians for their fiestas.

After using the back trails for a while, Andy discovered that the market was declared closed to him and his friends. Next, the elders denied him en-

Andy and his five-man combo were the town's musicians in the religious festivals until God changed his heart.

trance to the village and even his own home. Still they weren't satisfied.

"We all paid money for the band instruments, and now you won't play them," the elders cried. "You belong in jail."

That night the jailer borrowed a lock from Cal Rensch, who never dreamed it was going to bolt the door on his Indian friends.

For three days, the elders argued with the prisoners through heavy wooden bars. The new Christians held their ground. "We'll play for school fiestas but not for the images!" they declared.

Finally, on the fourth day, the elders said, "Let this teach you to follow the tribal traditions." And they let the band out of jail. "You have been disgraced," the elders said. "No one will listen to you now."

But the elders were wrong!

The Woollytown Five soon grew to seven and then to nineteen. They built a little palm thatched church. The elders burned it down. The Christians built it again and they won still others to their newfound Saviour.

Today 350 Chinantec believers meet in a much larger palm thatched church.

And Andy—well he still blows a trumpet loud and long, but he has better reasons than before. "The gospel has made me become sober," he explains. "I can think clearly for the first time in my life!"

Reprinted from *Looking Ahead,* © 1968, David C. Cook Publishing Co., Elgin, Ill. Used by permission.

Mexico

34

Part One

The Boy Who Whistles to Talk

The hoe handle he used was long and slippery, worn smooth from years of hard hoeing in the steep Mexican Mazatec Indian cornfields. Little Tino Cortés, with all the determination of his ten years, gripped the neck of the hoe and dug it hard into a tangle of weeds. In this Swiss-like section of Mexico, flatland does not exist. Most cornfields outside Tino's town of Huautla de Jiménez have been shaved from the sides of steep mountains. Some angled at sixty degrees. It was like hoeing weeds on a ladder with each row of corn level with your nose.

To keep from slipping out of the cornfield, Tino had to grip his bare toes into bumps and ridges on the mountainside. Before he moved up, down or sideways, he carefully removed one foot at a time.

Then like a spider, he reached out for a new position. Only after wiggling his toes firmly into a new clump of earth or a crevice did he shift his weight and begin to hoe a new patch of weeds.

By midmorning Tino was hungry, thirsty and tired. He had worked almost without stopping since before dawn. At the end of a row of corn, he decided it was time to rest. Using his hoe like a mountaineers axe, Tino dug it into the ground and pulled himself up through the budding cornstalks to a narrow mountain ridge.

When he reached the top, he quickly found his water jug hanging in the shade of a tree to keep it cool. With a jerk of his wrist he pulled out the dry corn husk used for a stopper. After three long, gulping swallows, he burped and gave a satisfied sigh of relief. Some of the water trickled down the side of his mouth and dripped onto his white shirt. With a dirty hand he wiped it from his mouth and rubbed it over his oval face. It felt good. He took in a deep breath of fresh mountain air and smiled to himself.

As he was ready to climb back down into the cornfield, Tino saw someone on the trail far below in the valley. For a long time Tino watched while the man climbed up the steep trail. Tino realized it was his Bible translator friend, George Cowan.

"Why," thought Tino, "would Señor Cowan come all the way from town to climb this steep trail?" Deeply curious, Tino wanted to shout and ask him why. But he knew Mr. Cowan was too far away to hear his voice.

Hoeing was quite a job. To keep from slipping, Tino would poke his bare toes into ridges in the steep mountainside.

Then Tino did a strange thing. He puckered up his lips and blew a long whistle that went up and down like notes in a scale.

Mr. Cowan heard the strange, clear whistle and stopped walking. "Ah," he thought, "I have found him. That's Tino's whistle."

Then just as Tino had done, Mr. Cowan puckered his lips and answered with another strange sounding whistle. Tino again puckered his lips and whistled. And for a third time Mr. Cowan whistled. This time he answered with a much longer whistle. When Tino heard this whistle, he clapped his hands together, grabbed his hoe and water jug and raced down the trail to meet his friend.

During the whole time Tino and Mr. Cowan were whistling to each other, not one word had been spoken. Yet Tino left his work and ran to meet a friend. The Mazatec Indians don't know it, but they are one of the few people in the world who can talk in sentences without using words. The Mazatecs can do this because their language is tonal. This means words and phrases in this Indian language are spoken with a musical pitch.

Using the numbers 1, 2, 3, 4 on words to tell us when to make our voice go up and down, part of Tino's and Mr. Cowan's whistle talk looks like this:

Tino's first whistle—"Where are you coming from?"
$Hña^1\ khoa^2$? $ai^4\ -ni^3$

Mr. Cowan answered—"I am coming from Huautla." Ni^3? $ya^2\ -khoa^2$? $ai^4\ -nia^3$

Tino then asked—"Where are you going now?"
$Hña^1\ ti^3$-? $mi^3\ nt$? ai^4

Mr. Cowan then gave a very long whistle and told Tino he was going to Mexico City. But the part that made Tino run so fast down the trail was when Mr. Cowan asked Tino if he would like to go to the big city with him!

Tino was so excited when he reached Mr. Cowan that his words, and occasionally his whistles, tumbled out all at once. Mr. Cowan laughed and held Tino's hands.

"Slow down! Slow down!" he said. But all Mr. Cowan could hear over and over again was, "When do we go? When do we go? What will I do there?"

"We will go tomorrow," answered Mr. Cowan. "And when we get to the city I want you to help me make gospel records. I will put your voice on a round plastic disc. When the Mazatecs play these (records), they will hear your voice talking to them about how much Jesus loves them."

Mr. Cowan talked about how they must get packed for the long trip. But Tino hardly heard him.

Never in all his life had he ever believed he would visit Mexico City. And tomorrow, he really, really was going!

Part Two

The Boy Who Whistles to Talk

When Mr. Cowan asked Tino to go with him to Mexico City it was because he had been observing him for many weeks. And he liked what he saw!

Tino was smaller than most Mazatec boys at ten. And because he didn't have a living mother or father, life was harder for him than most boys. His pants and shirt were more ragged and had more patches than his friends. Everyday his mean uncle made him carry his own weight in firewood up rocky trails. But this didn't seem to bother Tino and he did it willingly with a smile. "Because," he said, "I am happy to be a Christian and have Jesus as my real friend." And when most children complained about hoeing in the steep cornfields, Tino answered them back. Not with harsh words. With God's Word!

Every afternoon when he came to visit, Mr. and Mrs. Cowan taught Tino Scripture verses in his Mazatec language. Tino then memorized the verses by shouting them at the top of his voice while he hoed weeds in the cornfield.

But now Tino's enthusiasm for shouting was gone. They had started out on foot before dawn and walked up and down steep mountain trails. Tired and hungry, they arrived at their first stop by midafternoon on their way to Mexico City. It was just a small country Mexican village with a little two-story inn, restaurant and a single street of battered adobe stores and shops. But for Tino it was his first glimpse of civilization. He had never before seen buildings larger than his one-room adobe mud house.

"Come on," said Mr. Cowan gently. "Let's get something to eat."

With complete bewilderment, Tino paused a moment inside the door of the restaurant and looked around at the tables. Not just one like Mr. Cowan had in his house, but nine! And four chairs beside each one! On each table Tino noticed a little dish of chile sauce and salt and pepper shakers. "How very rich these people must be," he thought.

In a few moments after Mr. Cowan ordered their meal, a smiling woman in a brightly flowered dress gave Tino the biggest plate of food he had ever seen. Steaming black Mexican beans, hot tortillas and a thick, juicy beefsteak! Tino's mouth watered. He couldn't remember ever being hungrier but he waited until Mr. Cowan began to eat his meal. Tino didn't wait because he was being polite or was waiting for Mr. Cowan to thank God for the food. He waited because this was the first time he had been given a knife and fork and he didn't know how to use them.

Out of the corner of his eye Tino watched the way Mr. Cowan held and used his fork and knife. Then without a blink of his big brown eyes, Tino picked up his knife and fork and cut into his meat as if he had done it all his life.

After supper they climbed onto a big truck that took them to the train station. Tino had never seen a truck before and when they started down the road, poor Tino was so excited he lost his supper!

Nor had Tino ever seen a train before now. When the big black engine puffed, snorted and wheezed into the station just six feet away from where they

The little boy who carried water up the steep mountain made a gospel record in his own language in Mexico City.

were standing, he gripped Mr. Cowan's hand and wouldn't let go!

During the long train ride to Mexico City, Tino sat silently with his nose flat against the window-pane. Only once, after watching the red tail lights on trucks they passed, did he ask Mr. Cowan a question.

"How is it," he asked, "that the red fire on the back of trucks doesn't blow out in the wind?" Tino had never seen electric lights before and Mr. Cowan had a hard time explaining to him there wasn't a fire inside the truck's tail lights!

It was midnight when Mr. Cowan and Tino arrived at the hotel in Mexico City. Both were tired and dirty. Tino was barefoot, his hair tousled and both had dull brown trail mud splotched on their clothes. The man at the desk looked at them for a long time. Then he said, "I'm sorry. All the rooms are filled."

Mr. Cowan said that he was sorry too but he had written for a reservation. Reluctantly the man found his letter and with a flow of apologies, gave Mr. Cowan keys to a room.

The day for Tino had been so full of excitement and surprises it didn't seem possible that anything else could be more wonderful than the train ride. Except, perhaps, a ride in an elevator! When Tino and Mr. Cowan stepped into the little box-shaped room, Tino thought this was where they would sleep. But then the box suddenly zoomed up to the fourth floor. Little Tino hung onto Mr. Cowan just as tightly as he had when he first saw the train engine. Tino smiled when he got to the top. It was a great ride. But he wondered why his stomach felt funny.

"I think we should wash up," said Mr. Cowan when they got inside their room. Mr. Cowan turned on the tap and hot water came out, and Tino's eyes just popped! He jumped down from the chair he was standing on and looked under the sink for the fire. The only way water got hot in his village was by heating it over an open fire. And then only after it was carried up a long steep trail in a bucket!

But even more fun for Tino was the gurgling sound the water made when it went down the drain. Even after Tino was all washed and clean, he still wanted to fill up the sink and let the water out so he could hear the gurgle.

There were two single beds in the hotel room but Mr. Cowan suggested to Tino, since he had never slept in a bed, he might be more comfortable on the floor. For an Indian boy like Tino who slept on the cold mud floor of his Indian hut, the warm hotel floor with a rug would be a treat. "Besides," said Mr. Cowan, "you might get a crick in your neck sleeping in such a soft bed."

But Tino's answer to this was a big, "No!" This was his first opportunity to sleep in a bed. "I don't care if I get a crick," he thought, "I might never get another chance to sleep in a real bed."

Then without knowing how it happened, Tino and Mr. Cowan started to have a pillow fight. When it was over, Tino fell face down into the clean soft bed. In a moment he was asleep. It was the end of the most magical day he had ever spent.

Part Three

The Boy Who Whistles to Talk

Tino woke to the call of a rooster. He was used to the brassy rooster call in his village. For just a moment during the first drowsy seconds of waking up, Tino couldn't remember where he was. He thought at first he was home, but that couldn't be true. He had never been as warm and comfortable as he was now! When the rooster crowed a second time, Tino remembered. He leaped out of bed and pulled on his clothes. He looked for Mr. Cowan but the blankets on his bed were pulled up and he was gone. Tino didn't know it but Mr. Cowan had gone into another room to read his Bible and talk to God in prayer.

For a third time the rooster crowed. Tino went to the window and looked out. There between two buildings was a small courtyard. In one corner, seven or eight hens pecked and scratched in a tiny plot of hard ground. And perched on a skinny poinsettia branch was a rust-colored rooster flapping his wings, crowing and trying to keep his balance.

Tino finished looking at the chickens and decided to investigate the funny box Mr. Cowan called an elevator. The night before Mr. Cowan explained briefly what buttons to push when you wanted to go up. He also explained that because of a power shortage in the city, the hotel clerk asked them to walk down the stairs and use the elevator only when they want to go up to their room. Tino decided to look into this wonderful ride for himself.

When Mr. Cowan finished his devotions and discovered Tino missing from the room, he immediately went to look for him. He poked his head outside the door just in time to see Tino race down the stairs. In a few moments the elevator doors opened and Tino stepped out with a broad triumphant smile across his impish face. But before Mr. Cowan could call to him, Tino raced back down the stairs to repeat the action over again. Then Tino came up the second time. Mr. Cowan was waiting for him. It was hard to scold Tino but Mr. Cowan explained firmly why he shouldn't do this. But all Tino could ask was why wouldn't the elevator bring him down if it would take him up!

After a breakfast of hot cocoa with cinnamon and fried eggs on a tortilla covered with spicy tomato sauce, Tino and Mr. Cowan were off on another day of adventure. They were to go first to the recording studio. But before they went, Mr. Cowan took Tino in a taxi to the market to buy him his first pair of shoes. The night before when they took a bus from the train station to the hotel, Tino noticed the fare Mr. Cowan paiḍ. Now he couldn't understand why Mr. Cowan paid more money to ride in a small car and less money to ride in a "big car."

Mr. Cowan began to explain the difference. But when the taxi started to drive through the city, Tino lost all interest in his explanation. The tall buildings, tree-lined boulevards, people and fancy shops almost hypnotized him. To get a better view of the tops of buildings, Tino wound down the taxi window and almost twisted off his neck looking up at the skyscrapers. People walking on the street thought it was funny to see a little boy's head sticking out of a car window, with his eyes toward the sky, but Tino didn't care. He was having the time of his life!

Tino wanted to try out his new shoes which were open-toed sandals. So they walked back to the hotel.

"How do you like your new shoes?" asked Mr. Cowan.

"Ah, these things are hot," Tino said with a little scowl. But then his face brightened. "But I like the way they sound!" They squeaked when he walked!

Mr. Cowan and Tino arrived at the recording studio later that morning and began to record the gospel records. A strange sound appeared on the master tape. At first the studio technician and Mr. Cowan couldn't figure out where the sound was

49

coming from. Then they watched little Tino. Whenever it came time for him to repeat a Scripture verse, sing a song, or tell how he came to love Jesus, he wiggled his toes.

"There's our problem," said Mr. Cowan. "Tino loves that squeak and thinks everyone else should hear it too!"

"Well," laughed the technician, "the only way to solve the problem is for Tino to record barefoot."

But even after Tino took off his shoes, there was another problem. In almost every sentence a strange whistle sound occurred making the recording unclear.

"It's almost like he is whistling a couple of words in each of his sentences," said the technician.

"Well to tell the truth," said Mr. Cowan, "the Mazatecs sometimes do whistle to talk, but Tino is so nervous he's mumbling some of his words."

After Mr. Cowan explained about the Mazatec whistle language, the technician just scratched his head. "That's the most interesting story I've ever heard," he said. "But how are we going to solve the problem on the recording?"

Before Tino and Mr. Cowan started out for the recording studio on the next day, Tino knelt by his bed and prayed. "Lord," he said tenderly, "please help me speak clearly today because there are many of my people who are too old to ever learn to read Your Word. Help me to speak clearly so that these people will hear Your Word through the records and believe in Your Son, Jesus Christ."

The technician was just getting the microphone adjusted when Tino and Mr. Cowan arrived at the studio. "Good morning," he said cheerily. "I hope you have solved the whistling problem because today will be the last chance I have to work with you."

"Tino has prayed and believes the Lord will help him," said Mr. Cowan, "And a friend has suggested an experiment."

"Great!" said the technician. "Tell me about it."

"It's really very simple," said Mr. Cowan. "I'll stuff Tino's ears with cotton. When he begins to talk he will have to speak loud and clear to hear himself. Then if you turn the microphone around so that he is speaking into the back end of it, everything should work out fine."

"Sounds kind of funny to me," said the technician, "but anything is worth a try!"

"Well, Tino," said Mr. Cowan when they got back to the hotel, "what do you think?"

"I think Jesus is wonderful!" said Tino. "I am glad He heard our prayers."

"Yes," answered Mr. Cowan, "we really do have a wonderful Lord. And I'm glad He heard your prayer because now many, many hundreds of Mazatecs will hear God's Word through your voice."

So even though Tino sometimes still whistles to talk, the recordings are perfect and will be used for many years to come!

South America

How Old Is Nine?

Nine is a great age for a boy! A golden moment in time when his world is Stingray bikes, Little League in spring and football in fall. And hardly any responsibility in between—except maybe to make his bed, take piano or trumpet lessons and comb his hair. But sometimes, when he has to, a nine year old can be as responsible as an adult. That is, if he doesn't know he isn't supposed to be and lives in a remote Brazilian jungle.

At age nine, Timmy Graham didn't know much about Stingray bikes. But he did know about firesting ants because young boys in the Satare tribe in Brazil where Timmy lived with his parents had to put their hands into nests of firesting ants. This is supposed to make them strong, brave hunters when they grow up—only most boys faint with the pain. Timmy knew about football but he called it soccer. And when he was in his jungle home he never made his bed because he slept in a hammock.

Several weeks before it (the occasion for this story) happened, Timmy was outside a small store in the seaport town of Belem in northeastern Brazil. He was soon to board a riverboat with his family on the final leg of a very long journey to his jungle home. Timmy bought a soft drink called guarana. But before he was half finished, the small Amazonian riverboat gave a shrill blast on its whistle.

"That's the last call for all aboard," thought Timmy, "I better get going."

With a healthy gulp Timmy downed the last mouthful of guarana. Then like a frightened chameleon, he dashed across the hot road, up six cement stairs and down a long, heavy wooden pier. His brother, Stephen, half-worried and half-amused, yelled from the boat's stern. "Come on! Mother's mad at you for disappearing."

"Yes," said his older sister, Keren. "You're going to get it this time!"

"Aw," said Timmy, half out of breath scrambling up the gangplank, "this old boat never pulls out on time. Besides, who's in a hurry. It takes five days to get to Parintins."

Timmy was right. The blue and white riverboat didn't get away on time. And it did take five long days on the Amazon to reach the town of Parintins. He could have added that after Parintins they had a 48-hour ride across a lake so big you couldn't see the other shore. And then another four- or five-day journey up a river before they reached the Satare people. There was a Catalina flying plane at Parintins which could make the trip in minutes, but it kept to no schedule. It only stopped for a short time once a week in Parintins and the Grahams never knew when it was coming. The few times they happened to be there when the plane was there it was already full or going the wrong way.

Understandably, Timmy's parents were tired at the end of a trip. But for some reason they all seemed especially tired and grumpy after this one. Timmy couldn't understand it because on other trips the whole family made a game out of their long journey. No two trips were ever the same. Timmy and his dad often tried to see who could count the most sparrow-size butterflies. Or who would be the first to spot a monkey, macaw or long-clawed upside-down sloth. At night there were smoldering campfires along the riverbanks that looked like orange cat's eyes in the velvet darkness. Sometimes Timmy caught a glimpse of a tiny light bobbing up and down in the jungle. And he knew an Indian had made a torch by squeezing crude rubber into a ball, sticking it on the end of a stick and lighting it. Presto! The Indian had his own jungle flashlight!

Sometimes a free floating island, the size of a mobile home, would pass them and Timmy and his brother would pretend it was theirs and they were floating out to open sea. But even Stephen wasn't as interested in the changing scene.

When they finally arrived in the village all, except Timmy, flopped into their hammocks. The Graham house was like all the other Satare houses. A large platform built up on stilts, floor covered with palm bark, and a high peaked roof covered with palm thatch. To make the house as cool as possible, there were no walls or room dividers. They just tied their hammocks to the supporting roof poles and let the breeze cool them off.

The Satare Indians were happy to see the Grahams back. Many men of the small village were puzzled by the things Timmy's father told them about the true God and they wanted to understand more. But today they came just to visit and hear news from the outside.

Timmy's mother and father liked to talk and usually took every opportunity to speak to their Indian friends. So again Timmy was puzzled by their strange behavior. They hardly spoke to anyone. All they said was that they didn't feel well and had a strange feeling in their stomachs. Stephen and Keren complained of the same feeling.

"This must be a reaction to the trip," said Timmy's dad. "We should all be feeling fine in a couple of days."

But as the days passed his parents, brother and sister complained of not wanting to eat. The sickness that Timmy's dad said would pass in a few days, didn't! All of the Graham family, except Timmy, were severely ill with infectious hepatitis, a disease that makes you tired, grumpy, sick at the thought of eating and feels like the worst case of flu you ever had—only fifty times worse! Because

Timmy was the only well member of the family, he became doctor, nurse, caretaker and cook.

At first he felt important to have everyone dependent on his help. But by the end of the second week he began to wonder what was going to happen. So did Timmy's father. He, more than anyone, knew how serious their situation was. Often he tried to get out of his hammock and help Timmy. When he did he always said and did the same thing. "We've got to get out of here." Then he would look at his sick family and begin to cry.

"That's OK, dad," Timmy would say. "The Lord will help us. Don't you worry. Just go back to your hammock and rest."

Timmy didn't know it then, but hepatitis makes people deeply depressed. Big strong men as well as

It was five days on the Amazon, two days on the big lake and four more days up the river to Timmy's house.

small thin men cry as easily as a three year old.

But it was his mother that worried Timmy most. Every evening groups of Satare women came and sat around his mother's hammock carving balsa dolls and telling her how sick she looked. And telling each other it wouldn't be too long before she died!

By the middle of the third week, the situation was almost hopeless. The little family was hundreds of miles from medical help. Worst of all, no one back at the SIL center in Belem knew anything was wrong. The Grahams didn't have a radio because at that time the Brazilian government wouldn't give foreigners a permit to operate a two-way set. Then late one morning, when things seemed to be at their worst, Timmy heard the excited barking of dogs.

"Quit barking," he called.

"Hey, " said a voice in English, "that's no way to treat a guest and fellow translator!"

"Uncle Arlo and Uncle Dave!" cried Timmy excitedly. "What are you doing here?"

"In this part of Brazil, we were conducting a survey of other people who needed a New Testament translated into their language. Our director, Dale Kietzman, suggested it would be a good idea if we had the time to drop in and see you all. So here we are!"

It didn't take Arlo Heinrichs and Dave Fortune long to realize that the Graham family was seriously ill. Within hours the two men, with Timmy's help, packed the Graham's belongings, made a stretcher for Mrs. Graham and carried her to their waiting canoe. Powered with an outboard motor, they made the long trip back to Parintins in a record two days. But the trip was only half over. They still had five more days of travel down the Amazon to Belem.

When they reached the small jungle town of Parintins, they were amazed to find the Catalina loading for a trip to Belem.

"I am sorry," said the pilot after he heard Arlo's story of why they must get to Belem quickly, "but there is no room."

"Look," said Arlo, "these people are seriously ill. This boy has looked after his family all by himself for over three weeks. We must get them to the hospital in Belem."

"It's just impossible," continued the pilot, but before he could finish, Arlo looked the pilot straight in the eye, raised his eyebrows and said with a smile in his voice, "But you will just have to do it."

Reluctantly and against his better judgment, the pilot rearranged the cargo and squeezed Timmy and his family into the plane. Mrs. Graham was the last to board. Gently, Arlo and Dave laid her on the floor of the Catalina.

"Timmy," said Arlo, as they were about to take off, "you are on your own again. But don't worry. Soon you will be in Belem and in no time everyone will be well and healthy again."

Arlo's words were right. In a remarkably short time, Mr. Graham, Stephen and Keren were well. Even Mrs. Graham, who weighed only 83 pounds when she entered the hospital, recovered quickly.

And Timmy? Well, he just went back to being a nine year old in Brazil, watching football—oops—soccer and drinking guarana.

South America

Chaddy Walks Free

When I first saw Chaddy Stendal he seemed smaller than most boys at fourteen. But he looked more like Huckleberry Finn than Huck Finn himself! He had a generous supply of freckles splotched across his nose. His hair was bleached blond and it looked like it had declared war on all combs. He wore old blue jeans and a faded orange tee shirt. The only thing missing was a battered straw hat. He was fishing and his bare feet were tough and tanned. But instead of angling for catfish in the Mississippi, Chaddy was fishing for piranha in a lake in eastern Colombia.

I don't remember what kind of dog the original Huck Finn had, if he had one at all, but Chaddy's was a short-legged black Labrador retriever. While

Chaddy sat on an old log that jutted out into the cloudy lake, his dog, Trotsky, poked in and out of the shallow lakeside waters after some unseen object.

"How come Trotsky has such short legs?" I called.

"Something happened and he didn't get tall like he should," said Chaddy with a laugh. "But his short legs make him good for the jungle. My friend has a Geman Shepherd and his dog gets all tangled up in the vines."

Chaddy continued to cast his short line into the water.

"What's it like to fish for piranha?" I asked.

"Oh, real neat," he said. "I once caught a thirteen incher. That's huge for a piranha! They fight real hard and feel like a big fish."

"Are they really as dangerous as I have heard?" I asked.

Chaddy grinned. "Oh, I don't know. They don't bother you in this lake." He paused for a moment and said, "Unless you have a cut with blood on it. Then watch out! One guy, a tourist, lost the end of his finger."

"How did that happen?" I asked.

"Well," said Chaddy, "after he got the fish in the boat, he tried to grab it. But the piranha bit through the brass leader. When it fell, it flipped up and just snapped off the tip of his finger. Their jaws look like little bear traps and they keep snapping all the time."

"Wow!" I said. "I think I'll stick to trout fishing!"

"I imagine you've had many adventures living in

Colombia," I said when Chaddy finally came back to shore. "I heard you were once alone for four days in an unfriendly Indian tribe."

"Well, not really alone," said Chaddy. "Alfonso was with me."

"Who's Alfonso?" I asked.

"Alfonso is a Kogi Indian who lives with us all the time. He and I are just like brothers."

"Tell me about how you were stranded," I said.

"Well," he said, twisting a jungle vine, "our family works with the Kogi Indians. They live way up in the mountains of northern Colombia and aren't too friendly. In fact, the Kogis are famous for poisoning people. And when I got stranded there with Alfonso and we didn't have any food, boy was I scared!"

"But how come your mom and dad weren't with you?" I asked.

"Because it's so far away we have to fly into the village. This one time there were seven of us besides all the supplies, so we had to take turns flying in. My dad suggested that Alfonso and me should fly in first. When the little plane dropped us off and went back to pick up the others, the radio broke. Our mission has a strict rule that says no plane can fly unless it has contact with home base."

Sensing I was going to ask why, Chaddy answered my question before I asked it. "Because if it went down nobody would know where to look for it. I had a radio and found out from our home base that the radio on the plane had conked out. I knew mom and dad would come just as soon as they could. At least I prayed they would! At noontime the Indians didn't want to give us anything to eat. I was kind of glad in a way because I was scared they might poison our food.

"Then in the late afternoon I found my dad's twenty gauge shotgun and some shells in our supplies and Alfonso and I went hunting. In no time we shot six toucans."

"Did you know how to cook them?" I asked.

"Oh, no," said Chaddy. "We gave them to a Kogi family to cook and we shared the meat with them. Boy, were they excited! It's hard to get meat and Kogis get real hungry for it. All they have to hunt with are a few weak bows and arrows.

"After supper Alfonso and I went back to our house. It really wasn't much of a house. It was only half finished. I was a little scared because I thought there might be tigers outside in the night. I was only ten and didn't know too much about wild animals. Anyway, Alfonso and I boarded up the windows and closed in the door with boards and packing boxes.

"In the morning I wondered if the Kogis would be friendly and how we would get something to eat. Just when I was thinking all this, the Kogi man we gave the toucans to, came and banged on the house. 'Quick!' he said. 'There's a deer close to the edge of the village. Come and shoot it.' When I heard that I felt good inside. My dad always told me that if the Kogis ever come and ask for help or for a favor, then you can tell they have accepted you. And I knew then everything was going to be all right."

Chaddy (above) and his Indian friend spent three days alone with a hostile tribe before his parents arrived.

Everything was more all right than Chaddy or his parents ever expected. For the next three days Chaddy and Alfonso helped the Kogis clear land and work in their yucca fields. By the time his parents arrived on the fourth day, Chaddy was completely accepted by the Kogis. One night he even sat next to the chief in the secret council house—something his father didn't do until many years later.

Chaddy's parents finished their house and settled down to living in the village. But the Kogis always had a guard nearby. Whenever Mr. Stendal walked out of the house, a Kogi would ask where he was going. The only time Mr. Stendal could walk outside or leave his house unattended was to treat someone who was sick.

Because Chaddy was small for his age, the Kogis liked him. They didn't feel he could hurt them like they thought his father might. "We like Chaddy," said the Kogi chief to Mr. Stendal one day. "He is like one of us. And because Chaddy came first we have let you live among us."

When the plane's radio broke and Chaddy was stranded, Mr. Stendal thought he had made a great mistake by sending him in first. Now Mr. Stendal knows that God used his son to open the door so that the Kogis can have the translated Scriptures. "When we arrived in the village," said Mr. Stendal, "Chaddy had the Kogis all nicely warmed up!"

Before Chaddy wrapped up his fishing line and called Trotsky to go home, I asked him what he liked most about living in the village.

He gave me a big smile and his blue eyes twinkled mischievously. "It's fun," he said, "to have the tables turned and have freedom to do whatever an adult would do. Instead of Mom and Dad asking me where I'm going, the Kogis ask them where they're going! I can go wherever I want, but Mom and Dad have guards behind them."

Then as Chaddy walked up the trail from the lake, he called over his shoulder, "Better not come up to Kogiland. They might not let you out of the house! Come on, Trotsky, let's go home."

Mexico

Licha and the Evil Spirits

"Father," said Licha, "the stones near the water hole are covered with mud!"

Before Licha could continue, her father asked excitedly, "Did you fall?"

Licha, a 12-year-old Mexican Totonac Indian girl paused for a moment. Fear made her black eyes look very big. "Not only did I fall," she whispered, "I broke the water jug."

With a low groan, Licha's father slipped the machete he was sharpening into its brown leather case. "Come," he said. "We must satisfy the spirits that made you stumble."

Licha followed close behind her farther as they walked to a grove of orange trees. There several chickens were scratching for bugs. Expertly her father snatched up the fattest one.

"There. That's the place I fell," said Licha.

Without a word her father drew his machete and cut off the chicken's head. He then sprinkled the chicken's blood on the ground where Licha had fallen. As he did so, he called out, "Come back! Come back, spirit of my daughter Licha. Come back so she will not die. See, I offer this sacrifice to the spirits."

Satisfied that the spirits were paid off, they started home. On the way, Licha asked her father if she could visit the house of the white señoritas. "I cut my foot when I stumbled," she said. "It didn't hurt much then but it throbs now. They have medicine that can make it better."

Bible translators Ruth Bishop, Aileen Reid and Ella Marie Buttons ("Buttons" for short) were just sitting down for supper when Licha called to them. Licha rested her elbows on the heavy wooden dutch door and looked into the girls' large room.

"Please put medicine on my foot," Licha begged.

"It looks like a bad infection," Buttons said after examining Licha's foot. "You should have a penicillin shot."

Ruth carefully washed the cut with soap and water while Buttons prepared the injection. The needle pricked and Licha jumped. When the orange Merthiolate was dabbed on the open wound, she drew in her breath. But she did not cry.

"How did you cut your foot?" Ruth asked. When Licha finished her story, Ruth questioned her again. "Do you really believe that spirits made you stumble?"

"Oh, yes," answered Licha, her eyes wide with fear. "Everyone knows spirits make all bad things happen. Bad spirits made my baby brother die."

"Oh," said Ruth, "how did it happen?"

Licha brushed her sleek black hair out of her eyes. "One day," she began, "black clouds filled our valley. All of us wondered what would happen. Then Saint Michael drew his sword." (Totonacs believe thunder is Saint Michael drawing his sword.) "The noise of the sword came near our house.

"My father knew a bad spirit took my brother's spirit away because he cried all that night. Even the witch doctor could not get his spirit back.

When Licha slipped into the water hole and broke her jug, her parents thought the evil spirits had caused the fall.

71

Brother just became weaker and grew thin and coughed until he died."

"Licha," said Buttons, "will you listen while I read what the true God says in His Book?" Licha said she would and Buttons picked up a well-worn book. Then she pulled out a small three-legged stool and sat down beside Licha.

"A long time ago," said Buttons, "Jesus lived on earth. He wanted to show people that He was more powerful than all the bad spirits. So He did a wonderful thing for a man who had many bad spirits living inside of him."

Slowly and carefully Buttons read from the Gospel of Mark, chapter five. Licha leaned forward and listened eagerly.

After the story was over, Buttons talked to Licha. "Jesus can show you and your family that you don't have to kill a chicken and sprinkle its blood to satisfy the spirits," she said.

"You see, Licha, when Jesus, God's Son, died, His blood was spilled for us. He gave His life because He loves us and wants us to be free from fear. You can be free from fear if you tell Jesus you want Him to live in you."

Licha looked away. She stared for a long time at the rough, mud floor. Finally with a smile she answered Buttons. "I have already asked Him to come live with me," she said.

In the weeks that followed, Licha came to the translators' house almost everyday. There were so many new and exciting things to learn now about Jesus' way of life.

One day she surprised her parents by reading a

Scripture verse calendar the translators had made.

"How can you read this calendar when you have never gone to school?" demanded her father.

Fearing the anger of her father she told her story slowly.

"Little mother," said Licha's father after she had finished, "this is a good thing that Licha has told us. I would know more of this."

To Licha's great joy, her father kept his word. He went to the translators' home and heard God's Truth for himself. Then Licha's father asked Jesus to come and live with him too.

Licha's village of Appantilla remains much the same. Most villagers still get drunk at fiesta time. Many homes are made unhappy because fathers spend money for liquor instead of for food and clothes. Families still live in fear of evil spirits. Witch doctors still chant over the sick.

But Licha's home, like the homes of several other Totonac Indians, has been changed by the Spirit of Jesus Christ. Her father no longer comes home drunk. Money he spent for liquor he now spends for meat or shoes for Licha and the family.

Licha must still help weed the family cornfield, wash clothes, gather firewood and haul water. These will always be her chores because she is a Totonac girl. But now she has Jesus' love and help. Fear no longer rules her heart. Now she is sure of eternal life. Licha is happier than she ever thought she could be.

Reprinted from COUNSELOR. Used by permission.
Copyright 1970 Scripture Press Publications.

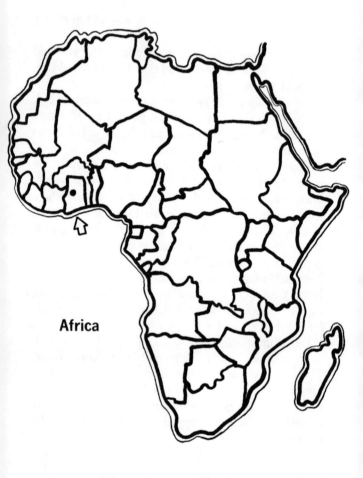

Africa

74

The Storm Was Over

It happened in May at the time of rain. The hot, dry winds that blew down from the Sahara and spread months of smoggy sand and dust across northern Ghana in West Africa had stopped.

Near the clay walled village of Jentilpe, leaves on the mango, dawa-dawa and baobab trees had just turned green—like the green of young, tender peas. Close-by two African boys worked in the peanut fields with their short handled hoes. Like other villagers, the boys started work before dawn to escape the blast furnace heat of the mid-day sun. But today the normally bright sun was hidden behind a pale, sickly sky that looked like watered down milk.

At first the boys were happy for the cooler day. But as the sky went from pale gray to gloomy black, they began to look at each other with worried glances. And when the wind rattled and shook leaves in nearby trees, the boys were frightened!

"Quick, run!" said one boy. "Mawu, the sky god, sends wind to warn us that he will come soon."

Frantically the boys raced home. Just before they reached their mud compound, the first drops of rain began to burst over their gray-black bodies. As they made a final dash for cover, two zigzag streaks of lightning flashed across the sky with the speed of a striking cobra. There was a moment of strange silence as if the whole world was holding its breath. Then the sound of thunder and lightning snapped, cracked and exploded in the distance like a thousand cannons firing at once. And as the rains came it was as if a giant poured out water from a never ending bucket.

In a while the rains stopped. When they did, children of the village ran out of their clay houses and splashed in the puddles. All except the two boys. It wasn't that they didn't want to have fun with the rest of their friends. But during the storm a baby brother was born into their family and the village elders wanted everyone in the family to watch while a chicken was killed to honor the new child.

The Vagla people of Jentilpe are animists. This means they believe rocks, hills, streams, wind, rain and many other things in nature can think, reason and have personalities like humans. Since this child was born during the time when the sky god, Mawu, came to visit them, they believed the child must have special powers.

Seven days after the baby was born, the village elders once again gathered for a special ceremony. This time it was to cut the tribal marks into the baby's cheeks, to give the child a name and prepare the clay mounds that would become his own personal gods.

With a sharp knife, two long crescent Vagla shaped marks were slit into the child's soft cheeks. From this moment everyone would know by this special mark that he was from the Vagla tribe. The Vagla people also believe a newborn child does not become a real person until he is seven days old. Only then can he be given a name.

The name selected for the new baby was Simindon. It comes from an African proverb and means "your friend is your enemy." This means the person who knows the most about you is the one who can harm you most.

There was one final ceremony to perform before the village elders left. That was to make the clay mounds outside Simindon's house which would be his very own personal gods. When he became sick or wanted special favor, Simindon's father was to kill a chicken and talk to the clay mounds. And each year on Simindon's birthday, a special sacrificial offering was to be made to the rain god. "If you ever fail to honor the rain god," said the elders, "then Mawu will send another storm and Simindon will die."

Simindon grew quickly and did all the things African boys have done for hundreds of years. He played leap frog and Ludo, a kind of African Chinese checkers. With grass woven snares he captured the funny yellow-headed lizards. And when he was seven or eight he went to work in his father's peanut fields.

Then one day, when Simindon was fourteen, an exciting and strange thing happened. He was sitting under the shade of a big mango tree when two young women drove up outside his walled village. Never before had he seen a white person quite so close. He thought it was fun to have such a different kind of visitor.

They spoke first to the village chief. "We are Bible translators," they said, "and would like permission to live in your village."

The Vagla chief looked puzzled and asked why they, of all people, would want to live in a hot place like Jentilpe.

"Because," answered the translators, "we have the words of the true God. We want to write them in a book so you and your people will know how much He loves you."

"But," said the chief, "none of my people know how to read."

"That is why we want to live here," said the translators. "We want to translate God's Word and teach you how to read and write in your Vagla language."

When Simindon heard the translators would teach the people about God and how to read in

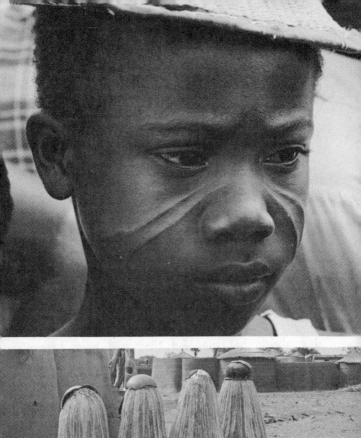

On his birthday a Vagla boy leaves a sacrifice by the clay
mounds which were built to be his personal god.

79

their own language, he became very excited. The dream of every African boy in Ghana is to go to school and learn how to read.

But more exciting to Simindon than learning how to read was the thought of knowing about the true God. He never told anyone before but he was beginning to wonder if the clay mounds and chicken or goat sacrifices really helped anyone. He noticed when his father offered sacrifices he never seemed happy. When Simindon asked his father about this one day, his father confessed sadly that he was never sure the sacrifices were going to work. "I just don't have confidence," he said, "that the gods accept my offerings."

After the two translators had been in the village several months and Simindon became their friend, he asked them a serious question one day about the true God they had been telling him about.

"I like the way you speak in my language," he said. "When you do I have confidence that you are one with me. But I have a question. Can you tell me the difference between the sacrifice I make with a chicken and the sacrifice of Jesus? I do not understand why He had to die."

"Let me explain by asking you a question", answered the translators. "When the Vagla chief does a wrong thing against the people of the village, what happens?"

"Oh," said Simindon, "you know the symbol of power for our tribe is a carved stool. Well, when a chief does a wrong thing, his stool is taken away from him. We Africans call it a destooling."

"And what does that mean?" asked the translators.

"It means," answered Simindon, "the chief no longer has power to rule."

"That's exactly what happed to man," said the translators.

"I don't understand," questioned Simindon.

"A long time ago man sinned. That is, he did a wrong thing against God who made all the things we see. And when man sinned he lost the power to live his life in a way that would make God happy.

"Now the only way God could ever be happy with man again was for someone to pay for what man had done. And because God really loves man, He sent His only Son, Jesus Christ, to pay for that sin. When Jesus sacrificed Himself on the cross He did it because He wanted to, not because He had to. He loves you and me very very much. Now, Simindon," said the translator, "do you deep down inside really believe the true God loves you?"

"Yes," answered Simindon quietly, "I do. I do with all my strength."

"Why don't you talk to His Son, Jesus Christ, in prayer?" said the translator. "You see, Simindon, Jesus is a real person and wants you to follow, obey and trust Him forever."

"This I will do," answered Simindon, and he bowed his head.

In the months that followed, the translators taught Simindon how to read the translated parts of the New Testament and how to grow in his faith.

On the day of Simindon's fifteenth birthday, his father, some of his uncles and the village elders wondered out loud why he didn't prepare to sacrifice a chicken and talk to his personal clay gods.

At first it was very hard to explain why he had not prepared. In fact he was hoping no one would notice. But since people of the village still thought the rain god sent him, they were very concerned for their own safety. Simindon should not forget to honor the god who was so important in making crops grow.

"I do not sacrifice a chicken this year," said Simindon nervously, "because I am now a Christian. The clay mounds are just earth and can no longer help me."

As Simindon continued to speak, the sky grew dark and gloomy. And just as it had on the day he was born, lightning cracked in the heavens, winds blew and the rain tumbled down. Like that day many years before, everyone ran for shelter. All except Simindon. He stood in the middle of the compound and let the rain wash over his graphite colored body.

Just before the last sprinkles of rain stopped, the villagers came out of their clay huts fully expecting to find Simindon dead, killed by lightning. When they saw Simindon alive and well, they didn't know what to do. Some were even angry that he was still alive.

"Please don't be angry," said Simindon. "Let me tell you how I became a Christian.

"Every year when I saw the feathers and blood of the sacrificed chicken, it made me sad. I didn't like it because I wanted a clean god. Then those who came to live among us and learn our language explained how the true God gave His only Son, Jesus Christ, to be our sacrifice. They told me God did this because He loves us all so much. And then when they told me that Jesus became alive again and wanted me to be His friend, I made up my mind to be a Christian.

"Since that time, when I put my confidence in Jesus, I have found that He guides my life like a lamp on a dark night. And because of this I don't ever want to go away from Him. I like to be a Christian!"

After Simindon finished speaking, many of the men, including his brothers, father and uncles, came to him. Some put their arms around his shoulders and asked him to help them discover Jesus.

In the distance the thunder coughed weakly. The gloomy sky divided and a thin layer of bright blue shone through. The storm was over.

Philippine Islands

Part One

Selanting

Something inside me said this time I would not escape. I think it was the way my mother called to me in the rice paddy.

"Selanting, Selanting! Quick! Quick, run! Hide in the jungle!" she cried. "The Philippine school police have come from the lowlands. They gathered your cousins and look for you to go with them to school in the lowlands."

I could tell when she said "quick" the police must be close to our bamboo house. And when she said they had already gathered my cousins, a hard sick feeling came into my stomach. Why, oh why can't the lowlanders leave us mountain Tagabilis alone, I thought.

But this was a time for action, not thinking. I ran and splashed through the muddy rice paddies like a frightened iguana. Once I tripped and fell on my face when I tried to jump a little mud dike. I cried. Why didn't the rope makers who sit by the village entrance not warn us? Before, when the school police came, they always shouted warnings from house to house. Since I live on the other side of the village, I knew they were coming before they reached our house. My mother then had time to wrap a big handful of rice and yams in a banana leaf and send me into the jungle. She told me to hide and not come back until dark. Always she told me the same thing.

"The lowlanders do not like Tagabilis. They will destroy your beliefs in our tribal ways. You will lose respect for your elders. You must not ever go to school," she would say.

Today I didn't worry about rice or yams. I thought only to get out of the rice paddy and into the thick jungle behind our home. My legs felt like heavy stones and my breath was heavy, but I kept running until I reached the edge of the jungle. Then I knew why the rope makers didn't warn us. The school police entered the village from a different trail and were never spotted. I ran straight into their arms!

The sick feeling came back into my stomach. I was caught! The school police would now force my mother and father to send me to the lowland school.

In a few days I left. When I did, my mother cried. She rubbed my lips, cheeks and forehead with a vine that clings tight to the giant mahogany trees. "Oh, god of the forest vine," she said through her tears, "as the vine follows the trees, so give my first and only son, Selanting, strength and wisdom to cling tightly to all that we have taught him."

It was hard to leave my mountain home. I felt alone and afraid. I was happy to help my father plow the rice paddies with our big carabao (water buffalo). And when rice planting time was over, I trapped monkeys and jungle rats in bamboo cages.

Others who had gone to the lowlands told me it would be hard. "Because," they said, "you are a Tagabili. You look different and wear different clothes." And on the first day of school it happened like I heard it would. The other children laughed at me. They pointed to my long hair and told me how messy it was.

"Why don't you comb it," they teased.

But I didn't have a comb and I didn't know how to buy one. They laughed at my baggy abaca-fiber pants. And laughed again because I didn't have pencils and paper like all the others. They laughed hardest when I didn't understand what the teacher said. His language was different than mine.

"Tagabilis are stupid people," said some of the older children. "They stand dumb like the water buffalo when you speak to them. And when they do talk, their language sounds like the chatter of monkeys."

Others told me I was stupid because I didn't know how to read or write and because there were no books in my Tagabili language. With sneers they told me I came from a minority group.

I failed my first year in school because I couldn't understand and I kept getting sick with malaria. And also because I was always hungry—I had food only once a day. When I was sick I could not go out into the fields to hunt for wild pineapple or coconuts.

When school was over I went back to my happy mountains. I hated school. I hated the lowlanders. But I knew I must go back. I had to show the lowlanders we Tagabilis are not stupid just because we look and speak different.

The second year was almost the same as my first. But when I went back to school the third year, my cousins told me news I did not believe.

"But it is true," they said. "The Melikan bukay (white Americans) now live by the lowland school. News from the market is that they are kind to us Tagabilis and learn to speak our language. People also say the white Americans are translators and want to write the words of God in Tagabili."

"Why do they want to do this?" I asked.

"They want to put them in a book they call the Bible. We also hear that they look for someone to help them learn our language. They say they will teach Tagabili people to read and write!"

I thought it strange the Melikan bukay were reported to be kind to Tagabilis when most lowlanders treated us like animals. So I thought to visit them. But it took three days to gather up enough courage to knock on their door. And when I did, I took my two cousins, Yadan and May, along to help me.

For a long time I stood outside their house with

Children in the highlands of the Philippines didn't know their language could be written until a Bible translator came.

89

fear in my stomach. When at last I knocked, a tall white lady with short brown hair came out. She was pretty and had nice teeth when she smiled. She asked my name. Her voice was soft and it made me feel comfortable. Suddenly I was no longer frightened.

I told her my name was Selanting, that I was a mountain Tagabili and that I went to the lowland school across from her house.

She asked me why we had come to visit her. I told her we had come to live at her house and go to school. When I said that, the white lady looked surprised. But I just kept talking.

"We are good workers and will look after your gardens and do the housework," I said. "And while we live here, we will teach you all about the Tagabili language."

The white lady told me her name and said I was an answer to prayer. I didn't understand and didn't think about what she said. Many months later I found out that Miss Forsberg was praying to her God for someone to come and do just what I asked.

I was happy she said yes. It almost came too easy! In the weeks that followed I found all rumors were true. Miss Forsberg and her friend, Miss Underwood, were kind to us and all the other Tagabilis who came to visit. I also discovered I was not stupid. Because everyday after school when my chores were finished, Miss Forsberg asked *me* questions.

We sat around a table on bamboo stools. On small pieces of paper she wrote Tagabili names for flowers, birds, animals, sky, earth, trees—everything!

She wanted to know how we Tagabilis said hello, good-bye and names we used for mother and father. All these things she put down on paper.

For the first time I saw my Tagabili language was like Spanish or Tagalog or English. "It is just that no one ever bothered to learn how Tagabilis say things," said Miss Forsberg when I asked her about this. I felt good inside when she told me. Later when Miss Forsberg read whole sentences in Tagabili, I cried because I was so happy. I wanted to shout and tell all the lowlanders that our language could be written. It was not monkey talk. And I was not stupid!

When I told Miss Forsberg, she smiled and said I should not be angry against the lowlanders. She said Jesus could help me not to feel bitter. She had told me many times before about Jesus. The first time she told me I laughed. "Who is this Jesus?" I asked. "I have heard about God, but never about Jesus."

She told me He was God's Son and He wanted to be my friend. Then Miss Forsberg asked me if I understood why she had come to the Philippines. I said I didn't.

"I came," she said, "because a long time ago God shared a great treasure with the world."

I asked her what that treasure was. "That treasure," she said, "is God's only Son, Jesus Christ. And you know, Selanting, people never give treasures away unless they really love the person they give it to. I need you to help me tell the Tagabilis this great story."

I told Miss Forsberg I was confused and did not

understand how I could help her. She told me I could help her put the words God spoke into my Tagabili language. She called this work Bible translating.

"The Book we call the Bible," she said, "is God's instruction to everyone. It tells us how to live and most of all tells us about why and how His Son came to earth. The Bible really tells us how we can all find everlasting life."

She told me what it means to follow Jesus. I still did not understand. But then she said some words that helped me. "When you follow Jesus Christ," she said, "you don't follow all kinds of rules. You don't have to pay money or hurt yourself. All you do is believe and obey Jesus. And when you do this you become a brand new person inside."

Her words made me think deeply. All of a sudden I understood why I liked her. And why the other Tagabilis liked her. It was this love of Jesus she talked about. I saw from the way she lived everyday that she really followed and loved this Jesus she called her Lord. I also understood that when I hated the lowlanders it really hurt me inside.

I told her I wanted to help, but asked her to tell me once again what happens when I follow Jesus.

"Let's read and find the answer together from God's own words," she said. "It is in that part of the Bible called 2 Corinthians 5:17. 'When someone becomes a Christian he becomes a brand new person inside. He is not the same any more. A new life has begun.'" (*The Living Bible.*)

When I returned to my mountain village after school was over, I was happy. Very happy.

"I don't understand why you smile and talk to the lowland people who come to buy rope," said my mother. "You know how they treat you when you live among them."

"I used to hate the lowlanders very much. But now I don't have to hate," I said.

She asked why. I smiled. "It is because inside a new life has begun!"

Part Two

Selanting

The first summer after Selanting understood how Jesus Christ could become his personal friend, he began to share his new life with other Tagabilis. Some like himself believed. And when it came time for them to attend the lowland school, Selanting took them first to the house of the Melikan bukay.

"I come with new friends of our Lord," said Selanting when he came back after the long school vacation. "All would like to live here with you and Miss Underwood. They need to know about Jesus," continued Selanting. "And they need to know that our Tagabili language can be written with letters just like Spanish or English. As you teach them they will help you translate more of the Bible."

Almost before they knew what happened, the two translators had five mountain Tagabilis boarding in their split bamboo house. Three of the new boarders were related. Bedung, a third grader, always wore a white V-neck tee shirt, long black pants and a quick smile. His younger brother, Kasi, wore a tee shirt but wore his long pants with the cuffs rolled up past his ankles. Their cousin, Fludi, was in the first grade. He wore short pants and went barefoot.

Life with the Melikan bukay was instantly happy. The boys attended the lowland school in the morning. In the afternoon they had a big meal of steamed rice, vegetables and fish. Later, when their light chores were finished, they practiced reading and enjoyed finding out how much God loved them.

Then one day something happened that made everyone in the house unhappy. It was late on a Sunday afternoon. Fludi and Kasi, with a group of other boys, were playing leapfrog under a big green mango tree. Fludi, with an extra spurt of speed, made a flying leap over Kasi and accidentally kicked him. Both boys fell over like doubled-up armadillos into a pile of turpentine-smelling mango leaves. Fludi and the other boys thought it was fun to roll on the ground. But Kasi didn't. When he picked himself up off the ground, his fists were clenched and his face filled with anger. Fludi didn't notice this at first and leaned back on his arms with a big smile. Then before he knew what happened, Kasi walked over and smashed Fludi in the face as hard as he could with his fist. Before the other boys could stop them, Fludi and Kasi were swinging and kicking all at the same time.

At breakfast the next morning it was Fludi's turn to thank God for the food. After he prayed, everyone was strangely silent and unhappy as they looked at him and were reminded of Kasi's quick temper. Poor old Fludi had the biggest black eye anyone had ever seen. And everyone realized that this was the first time any serious misunderstanding had happened since they all came to live with the Melikan bukay.

A few moments after Fludi prayed, Bedung cleared his throat and looked very stern. Then in a serious voice asked, "Fludi, have you asked forgiveness from Kasi?"

"But Kasi started it first," said Fludi with half a sob in his voice.

"But didn't you also get angry?" asked Bedung.

"Yes," said Fludi softly, "I did."

"And," said Bedung, "that is sin. God is not happy when there is sin in our thinking."

Fludi just lowered his head and picked at his food. In a few moments he left for school without a word.

In the evening it was Kasi's turn to thank God for the meal. When the food came, Kasi bowed his head and to everyone's surprise asked the Lord to forgive him for getting angry and hitting Fludi the day before. Then Fludi confessed to the Lord how easy it was for him to become angry and in a voice that really said, "I mean it," asked the Lord to help him get over this problem.

In an instant everyone seemed happier. Everyone but Bedung. His face was still stern and unsmiling when he opened his mouth to speak. "That was a nice prayer," said Bedung. "But I want to know if you have asked Fludi to forgive you?"

Kasi's big brown eyes were shiny with tears but he was smiling, "I have already," he said, "I have already." And then Bedung smiled, Fludi smiled and everyone smiled and ate the best tasting supper anyone could ever remember eating!

Part Three

Selanting

Selanting continued to bring not only younger children to the house of the Melikan bukay, but older boys as well. By the end of the fourth year there were five boys in grade school and six in high school along with Miss Forsberg, Miss Underwood and a new translator named Miss Porter who joined them because she wanted to help run the boarding school and learn Tagabili.

The translators now believed God has given them a new way to serve Him. They were surprised because they never dreamed they would be running a boardinghouse. But somehow this seemed to be the right thing to do. Most of the boys were beginning to follow the Lord and the boarding school was the ideal place to teach them how to grow and trust the Lord for everyday experiences.

One person who was just beginning to understand about being a Christian was May, a tall slim boy with shiny black hair and big round eyes. He was Selanting's cousin and, like all Tagabilis, had learned to smoke when he was a small boy. Tagabili fathers give tobacco to their children just like American mothers and fathers give candy to theirs. But since coming to live at the boarding school, May noticed none of the other Tagabili boys smoked. One day May asked Selanting why it was that he and the other boys didn't smoke like their fathers taught them.

"I don't smoke," said Selanting kindly, "because I want to have a clean body."

"A clean body?" answered May. "I don't understand."

"Have you never read in the Scriptures that our bodies are the home of the very Holy Spirit that God gives us when we ask Him to guide our life?"

"No," answered May, "I have never read such words."

"The words are found in that part of the Bible called 1 Corinthians," Selanting explained. "In chapter 6, verse 19 it says, 'Haven't you yet learned that your body is the home of the Holy Spirit God gave you, and that He lives with you?' (*The Living Bible*.) I believe this means that I should keep my body as well and strong as I can. Smoking makes it weak and I feel I cannot honor God with a weak body."

Selanting asked May if he wanted to stop smoking. May thought for a moment, shrugged his shoulders and said slowly, "Maybe I would." Then like a big brother, Selanting put his arm around May's shoulder and asked God to give May strength to help him stop.

But as the days passed the only thing that happened was that May stopped smoking in public. He still smoked when no one could see him. During the day May hid his cigarettes in his woven-palm sleeping mat or sometimes tucked in his belt or in his rolled-up pant cuff. But whenever he did this he wished Selanting had never explained why smoking was bad because even though he now felt smoking was a wrong thing to do, he couldn't stop.

One day just before it was time for the long school vacation, two things happened to help May

Mountain children lived with the translators in their homes. They did household chores and learned to read and write.

understand what following the Lord meant. The first was when his father came and took him to the market. In the excitement of poeple who shouted and called attention to the wonderful things to buy, May's father bought him three cigarettes. May thanked his father and tucked them into his belt.

When market was over, May walked back to the boardinghouse over the long dusty road. As he came into the courtyard he met Selanting and without thinking pulled up the bottom of his tee shirt and wiped the perspiration from his forehead. As he did, May remembered the cigarettes and tried to hide them by jerking down his tee shirt. But it was too late. Selanting saw them. At first neither spoke. In a few moments Selanting walked over to the shade of a tall palm tree and sat down. May followed. Then Selanting smiled and once again explained what it meant to follow the Lord.

Because he was embarrassed, May stopped smoking for a few days. But after a week passed he would sneak out at night and puff away on the cigarettes, out behind the tall coconut tree.

On the last day before school broke up for vacation, May swept the courtyard for the last time. When he was half finished it started to rain. As the great drops of heavy, Philippine rain exploded onto the stone courtyard May dashed into the house for cover. While he waited for the rain to stop, he picked up a Sunday school story paper and started to flick through the pages. A Bible verse outlined in red caught his eye. "All that is now hidden will someday come to light." (Mark 4:22, *The Living Bible*.)

Right then May thought of the times he had sneaked out behind the coconut tree. And he felt ashamed and miserable because he had broken his promise to Selanting and to the Lord.

The next day as he climbed up the steep mountains to his home, May thought about his cigarettes and wanted to smoke one. But then he remembered the Scripture verse. It kept going over and over in his mind. But May couldn't stand it and he reached under his belt.

When he told his story later to Selanting, he said, "As I climbed up the mountains my breath got heavier and heavier. Then all of a sudden I stopped climbing and reached for the cigarettes. But when I touched them I suddenly felt I didn't need them. I didn't even want my father to have them. So right there on the trail I told God I wanted His Son, Jesus, to live in my heart. I told Him that if He would help me I would keep my body clean so He would not be ashamed to live in a dirty house. When I said this my breath was light and I threw the cigarettes far into the canyon below. For some reason the rest of the climb was easy—and great was my happiness!"

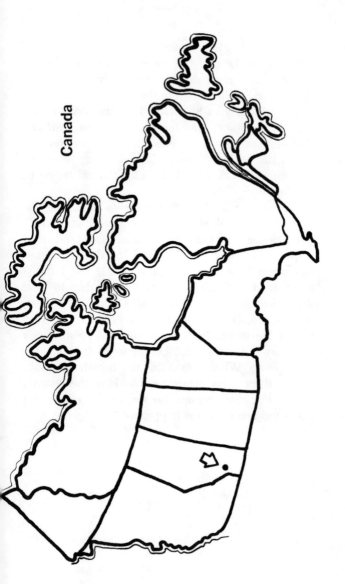

White Man Stoney

Expertly the Stoney Indian woman built a small fire of willow branches. Her hearth was an eighteen-inch hole at the base of an appaloosa-colored Canadian birch. Vigorously the flames ate at the dry tinder. But the willow branches were damp and difficult to consume. In frustration the flames died and the hole filled with a thick cloud of yellow smoke.

"Now," said Mrs. Georgia Two Young Man, "the smoke is right to cure the buckskin."

She was almost seventy but her movements were swift and decisive. In moments she arranged one end of a large square of fawn-colored buckskin over the billowing smoke. With the back of a three pound axe, she tacked the corners with wooden tent pegs. When this was done she tied up the remaining corners and drew the string up over a low hanging branch. Immediately the buckskin stretched into a four-foot funnel. With a quiet sense of satisfaction, Mrs. Georgia Two Young Man turned and spoke to the tousle-haired man beside her.

"Now, Mr. Harbeck," she said, "if you learn to make buckskin like you learn our language, you will be a good White Man Stoney!"

Sometimes when we see an Indian for the first time we think of buffalo hunting, Custer's last stand and Wild West shoot-em-ups. But when Warren and his pretty wife, Mary Anna Harbeck, see Indians they see them as friends and as people who have the right to speak, act and live the way they want to. They don't just see small clumps of white canvas teepees or unpainted two-room houses like most of us. They see a once-proud nation of people whose ancestors go back hundreds of years before white people came to live in North America.

The Harbecks don't think of the often one-sided view of a murderous villain that comes to us from bad T.V. serials. They think of a Plains Indian who used to show his bravery by walking into an enemy camp, untying the chief's horse and riding it out. (The horse was always tied right beside the chief's teepee.)

Warren likes to remind people that when the Indians first met the white man in battle, he didn't try to kill him. He tried to hurt the white man's pride by counting coup. This was a kind of ceremonial war game which gave high marks to the brave who touched his enemy with a special stick without killing him.

When I asked Warren and Mary Anna why they came to live among the Stonies, they gave me a look that seemed to say, "How could we do anything else?"

"We believe," said Warren, "that the Stonies, their cousins the Blackfoot, Crees and other groups in Canada and the United States, have been misunderstood and mistreated for a very long time. Part

The missionary was eager to learn how to make a good buckskin from the seventy year old Stoney Indian woman.

of my job as a Bible translator is to try and give to the Stonies the good feeling of being Indian."

"What kind of feeling is that?" I asked.

"It's that kind of feeling you get," said Warren, "when you hear the 'Star Spangled Banner' or 'The Maple Leaf Forever' and say in your mind, 'I'm glad I am American or Canadian' or whatever you are."

"How can you do all this?" I asked.

"There are a couple of ways," said Warren. "One is by showing honest concern and interest in the things that are important to them as native people."

"Like asking how to make buckskin?" I asked.

"Yes, exactly," said Warren. "You see the Stonies have been told they are 'no good,' or not as smart as Whites for so long they have begun to believe it. When I as a white person can honestly ask advice about how to do something, this makes them believe and have confidence in themselves as people.

"Another way to rebuild personal confidences and dignity," continued Warren, "is to respect the Stoney language. I want to tell the Stonies how much God loves them. I want to tell them in their own language."

"I have heard," I said, "that some people wonder why you should bother to translate the Scriptures into Stoney when English is taught in school."

Warren became serious when I asked him this question. He seemed to share the same feeling that the Indians have when they are asked why they don't learn English.

"English is an uncomfortable second language for most Stonies," said Warren slowly. "Often Stonies read English words without understanding what they mean. Or they will use English words with Stoney meanings. For instance, Indian men talk about cars as the thing that puffs out smoke. Or if a white man stares at an Indian he will say, 'Don't throw your eyes at me.'

"Many white people feel uncomfortable with people who are different and think the easiest way out of feeling uncomfortable is to get rid of the difference. Thirty years ago Stoney children were strapped by their school teachers if they were caught speaking their own Stoney language. But today there are more Stonies who speak their language than there were then!"

Warren and Mary Anna are just beginning to translate the New Testament. The Stonies love the few Scriptures they have translated. "Before," said Warren, "when we read the Bible in English, the Indians looked bored and uninterested. Now when I read the Scriptures in Stoney I hear the Indians agreeing with me under their breath. It is just like someone flipped a light switch in their minds."

Sometimes Warren gets discouraged with people who tell him he is wasting his time and his life working with the Stonies. When he does he always remembers the two Stoney government workers who thanked him for giving reading material and Scripture verses to their people. When Warren asked them why they wanted him to translate the Scriptures into Stoney, they both answered at the same time. "Because," they said, "Stoney is *my* language!"

Australia

The Meatless One

At first, Bible translator, Jim Marsh, thought the Western Australian outback looked just like the desert in New Mexico. It had the same kind of red hills, mesquite trees and tumbleweeds.

But Jim soon found Western Australia very different. "Most newcomers to our community of Jigalong don't realize how different and difficult this country is," said a police constable friend. "Those trees you call mesquite are called mulga trees. They're Western Australia's candy store."

"Candy store?" questioned Jim.

"Yep," said the constable. "They drip a kind of sweet red gumdrop. The aborigines just love it! Those desert dwelling aborigines are fantastic trackers and can live out in the desert on almost nothing. 'Course now we try to bring them into communities like Jigalong. It's too hard to keep track of them when they are wandering around the desert. See that tumbleweed?"

"Yes," answered Jim.

"Well, in America," said the constable, "they're a pesky plant. And they are out here too. But the aborigines tie them together to use as huts."

Then with a throaty chuckle, the khaki-clothed policeman said, "You have a lot to learn, young man, if you think this desert is like any other on earth. I remember the story of two men who went out into it and got lost. We sent a policeman and a couple of aborigines to track them down. They were found too late. They died of thirst. But the strange thing was, the aborigines dug a hole a few inches from where the men died and found all the drinking water they needed!"

"I wonder if making friends with the aborigines will be as hard as living in the desert," Jim said.

"Making friends with the aborigines!" exclaimed the policeman. "I don't know why you would want to make friends with them! Hardly anyone really understands or cares to understand what makes them tick. No white man I know has ever been their friend."

Jim gave his friend a good-natured slap on the shoulder and a big smile. "You're looking at one who plans to understand and love them as real people." Jim paused for a moment and then said, "And the reason I want to do this is because I know that's what Jesus Christ would do!"

It didn't take Jim long to put his words into action. A few days later he met a group of aborigine cowboys who spoke the Mantjiltjara language. They had rounded up range cattle from the surrounding desert and brought them into Jigalong. For some reason a young man about eighteen caught Jim's attention. He wore a greasy, rumpled cowboy hat pulled down tight over his eyes. It was hard at first to make out the young man's facial features. His skin was dark chocolate brown; his nose flat and broad. Then Jim noticed he had a wide smile and when he bent down a little and looked up under the young man's wide brimmed hat, he could see his dark eyes smiled.

Turning to one of the smaller boys who tagged along wherever he went, Jim asked him the cowboy's name. Jim knew it was considered rude and impolite to directly ask an aborigine his name. Jim also knew aborigines have two names. The sacred one given at birth which is known only by the father and a few older men, and a nickname which tells something about the person.

"His name is Kuwipani," said the boy.

Jim smiled when he heard the name. It meant, "The Meatless One." Still smiling Jim walked up and shook Kuwipani's hand.

It may be because aborigines are supersensitive to signs in the desert which mean his survival that he is also supersensitive to true honesty and concern in people. Kuwipani saw this in Jim and felt it in his handshake. He immediately trusted Jim as a friend!

Many times in the following months Jim camped with Kuwipani and his family out in the desert. Jim slept in the same tumbleweed huts and ate their kangaroo stew meat. And when there was no food left, Jim went with Kuwipani, his rib bulging dogs and other young aborigines to hunt the speedy kangaroo. Jim's weapons, like Kuwipani's, were carved hitting clubs, throwing sticks and spears.

There was always great excitement whenever a kangaroo was killed. Kuwipani was especially happy because friends didn't call him "The Meatless One" the same way they had earlier when he earned his nickname by missing too many kills! And Jim was happy because the aborigines from Jigalong accepted him as one of them. Kuwipani always introduced Jim to strangers and friends as, "This is Jim. He carries meat like an aborigine." At first Jim didn't understand this until one day, after a kangaroo hunt, he saw other aborigines smile and nod their heads in approval when Jim draped a dead kangaroo across his shoulders and start back to camp.

As Jim and Kuwipani camped together, Jim learned more and more of the Mantjiltjara language. And Kuwipani taught him some of the secrets of the desert—like how to dig for water that often lies a few feet below the hot, dry desert floor. Once when Jim's water tank sprang a leak, Kuwipani showed Jim how to fix it with an ancient aborigine trick. He took gum from the "black boy" plant and pressed it into the hole. The gum quickly hardened making a neat permanent seal.

Because Jim had proven his love and respect for the aborigines, they rewarded him by inviting him to share in the "men only" business of the aborigines' council and explain why he had come to Jigalong. Jim explained how God sent His only Son into the world to live among men. How Jesus Christ loved all men and paid a great price on the cross to give them freedom from sin, selfishness and eternal punishment. Jim also explained that he had come to share this great story and put it in a book so they all could understand and read it for themselves. "Because," said Jim, "the words I speak are not my own. They are God's words and you should know what He has to say to you."

All during the time Jim spoke, Kuwipani lay with his hands folded behind his head and smiled brighter than when he first met Jim. Jim smiled too because he thought how great it was that he had a friend like Kuwipani who could become his trans-

The translator learned secrets of the desert and the Mantjiltjara language from an Australian aborigine cowboy.

lation helper. Jim knew Kuwipani had not openly believed in Jesus and he couldn't be sure if he believed at all. "But," thought Jim, "just as soon as he begins to read and study the translated portions of Scripture, I know the Holy Spirit will help him to understand."

But that never happened. Soon after that unusual meeting under the mulga tree, Jim left Jigalong for the big city of Darwin. Business and other duties kept him from returning to Jigalong for many months.

One day Jim received a letter from his policeman friend. "I know you would want to know," the letter said. "I am deeply sorry to tell you that Kuwipani is dead."

There were other words but Jim couldn't see them. His eyes blurred. Silently he found the shade of a tree and sat down.

"He died still hungry," Jim thought. "I'll never know if he fully understood how much God loved him."

When Jim returns to Jigalong he will weep with Kuwipani's widow and as is their custom he will never speak Kuwipani's name in public for many, many years.

Jim will honor the customs of the Mantjiltjara because he loves and respects them as people. And because he loves them, Jim will willingly spend long, hard hours translating the New Testament into their language. He knows there are many more aborigines in Western Australia's outback. He doesn't want them to die like the Meatless One—still hungry!